An animated version of this book, together with four other stories by Tony Ross, is available from Tempo Video.

British Library Cataloguing in Publication Data
Ross, Tony
  I want my potty.
  I. Title
823'.914 [J]

ISBN 0-86264-137-3

© 1986 by Tony Ross.
First published in 1986 by Andersen Press Ltd., 20 Vauxhall Bridge Road,
London SW1V 2SA. Published in Australia by Random House Australia Pty., Ltd.,
20 Alfred Street, Milsons Point, Sydney, NSW 2061. All rights reserved.
Colour separated in Switzerland by Photolitho AG, Gossau, Zürich.
Printed and bound in Italy by Grafiche AZ, Verona.

I Want My Potty

Tony Ross

Andersen Press · London

"Nappies are YUUECH!" said the little princess.
"There MUST be something better!"

"The potty's the place," said the queen.

At first the little princess thought the potty was
worse.

"THE POTTY'S THE PLACE!" said the queen.

So . . . the little princess had to learn.

Sometimes the little princess was a long way from the potty when she needed it most.

Sometimes the little princess played tricks on the potty . . .

. . . and sometimes the potty played tricks on the little princess.

Soon the potty was fun

and the little princess loved it.

Everybody said the little princess was clever and
would grow up to be a wonderful queen.

"The potty's the place!" said the little princess
proudly.

One day the little princess was playing at the top of
the castle . . . when . . .

"I WANT MY POTTY!" she cried.

"She wants her potty," cried the maid.

"She wants her potty," cried the king.

"She wants her potty," cried the cook.

"She wants her potty," cried the gardener.

"She wants her potty," cried the general.

"I know where it is," cried the admiral.

So the potty was taken as quickly as possible

to the little princess . . . just

. . . a little too late.